For Linda and Matthew,
with love ~ J.F.

First published 2004 by Walker Books Ltd
87 Vauxhall Walk, London SE11 5HJ

2 4 6 8 10 9 7 5 3 1

This book has been typeset in Granjon

Printed in China

British Library Cataloguing in Publication Data:
a catalogue record for this book is available
from the British Library

ISBN 0-7445-9654-8

www.walkerbooks.co.uk

WALKER BOOKS
AND SUBSIDIARIES
LONDON • BOSTON • SYDNEY

WATCH OUT, WILF!

by Jan Fearnley

Wilf was a little brown mouse, bright as a button and full of fun. He loved to run and skip, and climb and play, and jump about. From the moment the sun filled the sky, till it dozed against the hillside, Wilf was full of busy. His mum was pretty busy, too – *and* she had to keep up with Wilf!

One day, when Wilf was busy running, his mum said, "Watch out, Wilf! Mind where you're going!"

Now, Wilf was a good boy.
He wanted to listen to his mum,
he really, really did …

but he was so busy running
he didn't hear her!

"Look at me, Mum!"
shouted Wilf.

"I can go fast!
I'm like a
whirlwind!"

He went faster and faster and ...

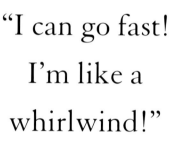

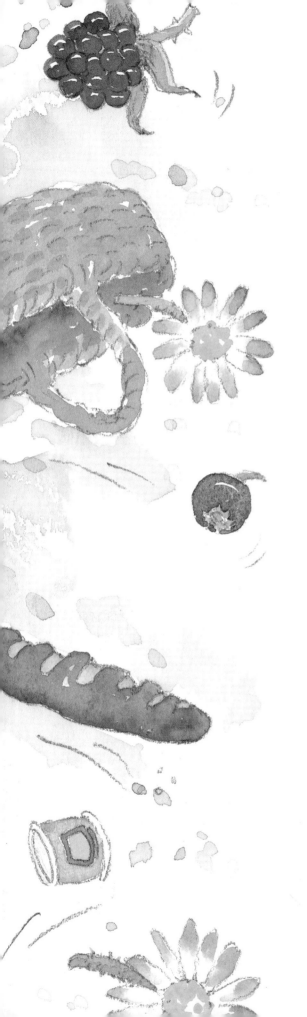

"Oh, Mummy!" said Wilf.

"Oh, Wilf," said Mum.

"I wish you'd listen to me."

Not five minutes later, Wilf was at it again.
This time he was climbing up the flowers,
even though they were still wet
from the morning dew.

"Watch out, Wilf!" said Mum.

"Don't dangle from the dahlias."

But Wilf didn't hear her ...

he was
too busy
climbing!

"Look at me!" he cried.
"I'm like a little monkey!"

"I can
climb
and climb
and climb
and..."

CRASH
BANG

WALLOP!

"Owww, Mummy!" said Wilf.

"Oh, Wilf," said Mum.

"I wish you'd listen to me."

Now Mum needed to do some baking.

Wilf was helping.

"Watch what you're doing with that honey," said Mum.

"We don't want it stuck on your whiskers, do we!"

But Wilf didn't hear her.
He was already away,
busy stirring the big pot
of shiny, yellow,
glossy
honey

round
and
round
and ...

CRASH BANG WALLOP!

Over went the table.
Over went the honey
– all over Wilf.

"Oh, Mummy!" said Wilf.

"Oh, Wilf," said Mum, as
she got the Wet Flannel out.

"I wish you'd listen to me."

It was getting late and Wilf's busy day was nearly at an end. But just before supper, Wilf decided to do some jumping about in the garden.

"Watch out, Wilf!" said Mum.
"Do try to be sensible. It's very muddy."

But Wilf didn't hear.
He was already busy
– busy jumping about!

"Look at me!"
he shouted.

"I'm a wild thing!
I'm a crazy kangaroo!

I'm a
bouncy frog!

Bouncy,
bouncy,
bouncy…"

SPLISH SPLASH WALLOP!

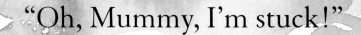

"Oh, Mummy, I'm stuck!"

"Oh, Wilf!" said Mum.

"This is a Fine Mess!

There's too much crashing and banging and not enough listening. I wish you'd slow down, my lad!"

After Wilf had taken his bath,

Mum sat in her chair and had a little rest.

Wilf had a little think.

He loved his mummy very much

and he didn't like her to be sad.

He decided to make a surprise to cheer her up.

Very quietly (so Mum wouldn't hear),

Wilf sneaked into the kitchen and made himself busy.

He made a pretty card.

He set a tray with a nice bit of supper.

It was beautiful!

Wilf couldn't wait to surprise his mum.
He took his time and was ever so careful

in the kitchen …

down the hall …

right to Mum in the big chair.

"Surprise!"

he cried proudly. "I made this for you!"

Mum opened her eyes, sat up and clapped her paws.

"Oh, my sweet boy," she cried, reaching out to Wilf.

"Come and give your mum a cuddle!"

"Watch out, Mum!" said Wilf. "Everything's wobbling!"

But Mum didn't listen!
She was too busy wanting
her cuddle and ...

I love you
mummy

… went the surprise.

"Oh, Mummy," said Wilf.

"Oh, Wilf," said Mum.

"Why didn't I listen to YOU!"

It was a terrible mess, but nobody minded.

"I'd still like my cuddle, if that's OK," whispered
Mum. And that is exactly what she got,
because this time, Wilf heard
every single word she said.